"Bring The Classics To Life"

The Pioneers

LEVEL 4

Series Designer
Philip J. Solimene

Editor
Laura M. Solimene

Cover Art
Matthew Archambault

Black & White Illustrations
Ken Landgraf

EDCON PUBLISHING
Long Island, New York

Story Adapter
Annie Laura Smith

Author
James Fenimore Cooper

About the Author

James Fenimore Cooper was born in Burlington, New Jersey in the year 1789. He was educated at Yale, and later joined the Navy. He began his writing career, by chance, when he and his wife were reading a novel together. James boasted that he could write a better book than the one they were reading. His wife challenged him, and James accepted the challenge. His first book, *Precaution* (1820), was not successful, but his second, *The Spy*, written the following year, received great reviews. Some of his novels include *The Pilot* (1823), *The Last of the Mohicans* (1826), *The Prairie* (1827), and *The Red Rover* (1828). He also authored *The Pioneers, The Pathfinder*, and *The Deerslayer*, the three of which are known as the Leatherstocking series. His daughter, Susan Fenimore Cooper, wrote *Rural Hours* in 1850, a year before her father's death.

Copyright © 2020, 2008
Remedia Publications Inc.
Edcon Publishing Group, Inc.
Scottsdale, Arizona

All rights reserved. No part of this book may be reproduced in any form or by any means, electronic or mechanical, including photocopying, recording, or by any information storage and retrieval system without permission of the publisher, with the following exception:

Student activity pages are intended for reproduction. Remedia Publications grants to individual purchasers of this book the right to make sufficient copies of reproducible pages for use by all students of a single teacher. This permission is limited to an individual teacher, and does not apply to entire school systems.

customerservice@rempub.com

www.rempub.com

Printed in U.S.A.
10 ISBN # 1-55576-358-8
13 ISBN #9-781555-763589

CONTENTS

WORDS USED

Story 81	Story 82	Story 83	Story 84	Story 85
KEY WORDS				
buck	accident	friendship	action	claim
leather	area	future	peace	reminded
reins	hut	God	purpose	skill
rifle	servant	guests	settle	spent
settler	shoulder	mistress	sheriff	sugar
stocking	wound	pray	turkey	suggested
NECESSARY WORDS				
ambush	bullet	forbid	appoint	annual
cloak	herb	fuel	guilty	assistant
concern	instrument	grace	lawyer	click
descend	minister	service	responsibility	sap
quarry	treatment		sermon	
venison				

WORDS USED

Story 86	Story 87	Story 88	Story 89	Story 90
KEY WORDS				
accept	August	arrest	comfort	death
agree/agreed	greet/greeted	court	duty	lightning
pigeons	January	information	jail	pioneer
pride/prided	leap/leaped	officer	objected	shawl
rough	protection	person	perfect	thunder
spear	sight	prison	prisoner	tore
NECESSARY WORDS				
bass	justice	document	conscience	adopted
bridle	leash	miner	jury	crackling
challenge (d)	panther	mining	oxen	graves
recover (ed)	perch	native	trial	pardon
thrown		offense		slick
		ore		

CTR 409-81

A Cold Winter's Day

PREPARATION

Key Words

buck	(buk)	a male deer *The hunter saw four buck in a herd of deer.*
leather	(leŦH´ ər)	material made from the skin of animals *Brandon wore a leather coat to keep himself warm.*
reins	(rānz)	straps that are attached to a bit and used to guide an animal *The wagon driver held tightly to the horses' reins.*
rifle	(rī´ fəl)	a gun with a long barrel *The farmer aimed his rifle at the horse thief.*
settler	(set´ lər)	someone that settles (makes his home in a new country) *The settler built a log cabin by the river.*
stocking	(stok´ ing)	a covering of wool, cotton, silk, etc. for the foot and leg *Andy's stockings kept his feet and legs warm.*

A Cold Winter's Day

Necessary Words

ambush (am´ bu̇sh) a place where one hides in the hopes of surprising an animal or an enemy

The General told his men to take ambush in the woods.

cloak (klōk) a loose piece of outer clothing, like a cape, usually without sleeves

Dan wore a cloak to the costume party.

concern (kən sėrn´) a troubled interest or caring

Betty showed concern for her sick friend by bringing her some chicken soup.

descend (di send´) to come down from a higher place

The plane began to descend shortly after take-off.

quarry (kwôr´ ē)

1. an animal chased in a hunt; prey

   The hunter looked for his quarry in the forest.

2. a place where stone has been dug or blasted out for use in building

   Mr. O'Hara works in the quarry sorting stones.

venison (ven´ ə sən) the flesh of a deer eaten as food; deer meat

The hunters prepared the venison for their dinner.

People

Marmaduke is the Judge's first name. Sometimes he is called Duke, or Marmaduke.

Monsieur Le Quoi is a man who left France after King Louis XVI had been killed. Many Frenchmen had left France and found safety in America. Monsieur Le Quoi was one such man. He owns a store in town. He sells goods to the settlers.

A Cold Winter's Day

Judge Temple fires his rifle at a buck.

Preview:
1. Read the name of the story.
2. Look at the picture.
3. Read the sentence under the picture.
4. Read the first three paragraphs of the story.
5. Then answer the following question.

You learned from your preview that

____a. the Judge did not know how to use a rifle.
____b. the Judge's rifle did not work.
____c. the Judge killed a squirrel with his first shot.
____d. the Judge tried to kill a buck.

Turn to the Comprehension Check on page 10 for the right answer.

Now read the story.
Read to find out what Judge Temple shot with his rifle.

A Cold Winter's Day

In New York, on a cold Christmas Eve day in 1793, a sleigh moved slowly up the narrow mountain road. Judge Marmaduke Temple and his daughter Elizabeth rode in the sleigh pulled by bay horses. The Judge wore a heavy coat edged in fur. A cap with sides pulled down covered his ears. His daughter was bundled up in a man's cloak. Suddenly, loud sounds came from the forest.

The Judge called to the black driver, "Hold up, Aggy. The Leather-stocking has put his hounds into the hills. This clear day they have started their game." He looked up the road and pointed. "There are deer track a few steps over there." The driver pulled on the reins to stop the horses.

Temple got out of the sleigh and took a rifle from among the trunks in the back. A fine buck ran in the path near him. The Judge put his gun up and fired. The deer dashed forward. The Judge fired the rifle again, still not hitting the buck. The sound of another shot rang out. The buck flew into the air. Then another shot sounded through the forest. When the buck fell back to earth, two men appeared from behind the pines.

The Judge cried, "Natty, had I known you were in ambush, I should have not fired on this quarry."

"No, no, Judge," returned the old hunter, stepping out of the pines. "You used your gun only to warm your nose this cold day. Your gun would not have killed this quarry, even from an ambush."

The old hunter, Nathaniel (Natty) Bumppo, called Leather-stocking by the settlers, was a tall man. He wore a cap made of fox skin over his sandy-colored hair. His deer-skin coat was belted close to his body. He wore long, leather stockings. These leather stockings were clipped to his pants.

Judge Temple and the old man talked about who killed the deer. The young hunter with Leather-stocking pointed out four holes in a tree. These holes were made by the Judge's rifle.

"And the fifth?" the Judge asked.

The young man opened his cloak. Blood ran from his side. Judge Temple showed concern by offering to take the young hunter to the doctor in the village.

The young man refused to go. Judge Temple then offered to buy the deer, but the man shook his head and replied, "I have need of the venison."

"This money would *buy* lots of venison," said the Judge.

Elizabeth now showed her concern, too. She wanted to take the young man to the village for help. When he finally said he would go with them, Leather-stocking refused to go.

The horses drew the sleigh over the mountain toward the village. A lake, locked in cold for the winter, looked like a snowy plain. The village of Templeton stood at the foot of the lake. Judge Temple's large home of stone towered over the settlers' homes. Smoke poured out from the chimneys of his house.

As they made their way alongside a quarry, a four-man sleigh came fast up the mountain. The two sleighs were close upon each other before either was seen.

The four-man sleigh, drawn by four horses, drew nearer. Its driver shouted, "Draw up in the quarry or I shall never be able to pass you!"

Both drivers stopped their horses. The four men inside the large sleigh got out and greeted the Temples. When the two sleigh drivers tried to turn the four-man sleigh, it leaned over the edge of the mountain road.

The Judge exclaimed, "They will all be killed!" Elizabeth gave a loud cry. The young man traveling with them got out of the sleigh. He took hold of the reins. He turned the horses around so they could descend to the village.

The driver of the large sleigh was Richard Jones. He was Aggy's master. Jones saw the buck on Mr. Temple's sleigh. He told the group about his own killing of a deer.

Aggy spoke up. "Natty Bumppo fired the other gun. You know, sir, all the people say Natty kill him."

Jones said, "They lie..." He spoke to the black driver, Aggy, and reminded him of *his* side of the story. Aggy was afraid of his master, so he listened to his master tell about his shooting.

"Well, well, 'Duke will say no more about my deer. The Judge fired both barrels. He hit nothing but a poor young man who was behind a pine tree."

The Judge left Aggy on the mountain to help Jones fix his sleigh. Marmaduke made room for the others in his sleigh. Monsieur Le Quoi, Major Hartmann, and Mr. Grant got into the sleigh.

Judge Temple then took the reins of his sleigh to descend the mountain to Templeton. After his sleigh was fixed, Jones took the reins and began to descend the mountain, too, with sleigh bells ringing.

CTR 409-81

A Cold Winter's Day

COMPREHENSION CHECK

Preview Answer:
d. the Judge tried to kill a buck.

Choose the best answer.

1. This story opens on
   ____a. a cold Easter morning.
   ____b. Thanksgiving Day.
   ____c. Christmas Eve day.
   ____d. Elizabeth's birthday.

2. What were the sounds that Temple heard that made him tell Aggy to stop the sleigh?
   ____a. Running Deer
   ____b. Running Horses
   ____c. Leather-stocking's hounds
   ____d. Gun shots

3. When Temple saw deer tracks,
   ____a. he took out his rifle.
   ____b. he took out his bow and arrow.
   ____c. he covered the tracks to keep the deer safe.
   ____d. he sent Aggy into the woods to kill the deer.

4. Natty Bumppo was called Leather-stocking because
   ____a. he liked the name.
   ____b. he wore leather shoes.
   ____c. he kept leather in his stockings.
   ____d. he wore leather stockings.

5. Judge Temple had missed the buck, but he shot
   ____a. Leather-stocking.
   ____b. the young man who was with Leather-stocking.
   ____c. a buffalo.
   ____d. a goat.

6. First the Judge fired at a buck. Then Natty and a young man appeared from behind some trees. Next,
   ____a. the buck flew into the air after being hit.
   ____b. Leather-stocking's friend pointed out four holes in a tree.
   ____c. Leather-stocking's friend showed that he had been shot.
   ____d. Abby took off with the sleigh.

7. Who was driving the four-man sleigh that came fast up the mountain?
   ____a. Barnaby Jones
   ____b. Tom Jones
   ____c. Marmaduke
   ____d. Aggy's master

8. Old Leather-stocking kills animals for
   ____a. fun.
   ____b. food.
   ____c. their fur.
   ____d. their food and fur.

9. Another name for this story could be
   ____a. "A Young Hunter is Shot."
   ____b. "Sleigh Bells."
   ____c. "The Hunt."
   ____d. "Going Home."

10. This story is mainly about
   ____a. life in the mountains.
   ____b. the dangers of hunting.
   ____c. how a young man came to be shot.
   ____d. why Abby was afraid of his master.

Check your answers with the Key on page 67.

This page may be reproduced for classroom use.

A Cold Winter's Day

VOCABULARY CHECK

buck	leather	reins	rifle	settler	stocking

I. Sentences to Finish
Fill in the blank in each sentence with the correct key word from the box above.

1. The cat scratched at Mother's leg and put a hole in her ____________.
2. Mark aimed his ___________ at the wild bear coming near.
3. With a single shot, the hunter brought down the ___________.
4. "Has anyone seen my ___________ belt?" asked Sam.
5. The English __________ found life hard in the New World.
6. "Hold on to the _________, or you'll fall off the horse," said Father.

II. Making Sense of Sentences
Put a check next to YES if the sentence makes sense. Put a check next to NO if the sentence does not make sense.

1. Marie called a ***settler*** when her car hit a dog. ____YES ____NO
2. Josephine has a run in her ***stocking***. ____YES ____NO
3. Ralph's ***leather*** gloves keep his hands warm. ____YES ____NO
4. Andy chased the ***buck*** deep into the woods. ____YES ____NO
5. Mother always says when it ***reins*** it pours. ____YES ____NO
6. George's ***rifle*** helped put the baby to sleep. ____YES ____NO

Check your answers with the Key on page 69.

This page may be reproduced for classroom use.

CTR 409-82

The Homecoming

PREPARATION

Key Words

accident (ak´ sə dənt) something harmful or unlucky that happens unexpectedly (not planned)
Reggie was in a car accident last night.

area (âr´ ē ə) a spot, space, or place
The doctor said to keep the area around the cut clean and dry.

hut (hut) a small, roughly built house or dwelling (a place where someone lives)
The old man lived in a hut made of straw.

servant (sėr´ vənt) someone working in a house for pay
Mrs. Watson's servant takes good care of the house.

shoulder (shōl´ dər) a part of the body to which an arm is attached
Larry's shoulder hurt from carrying his backpack.

wound (wünd)
1. a hurt or injury caused by cutting, stabbing, shooting, etc.
   Jessie's wound needed to be treated by a doctor.
2. to cause a hurt or injury to someone or something
   Jeff didn't mean to wound the rabbit.

The Homecoming

Necessary Words

bullet (bu̇l´ it) a piece of lead fired from a rifle or gun
The deer was killed by a single bullet.

herb (ėrb ***or*** hėrb) any plant with leaves or stems used in medicine and food
Martha uses nothing but fresh herbs in her cooking.

instrument (in´ strə mənt) a small tool
The doctor uses an instrument to listen to your heart.

minister (min´ ə stər) one in charge of a church
The minister married Ralph and Linda this morning.

treatment (trēt´ mənt) the act or process of helping to make well
Ned tried a new treatment for his cold but, so far, it hasn't helped.

CTR 409-82

The Homecoming

"My shoulder wound is not serious," said the young hunter, entering the room.

Preview:

1. Read the name of the story.
2. Look at the picture.
3. Read the sentence under the picture.
4. Read the first four paragraphs of the story.
5. Then answer the following question.

You learned from your preview that Judge Temple

____a. had sent for a doctor.
____b. had gone to the doctor's.
____c. had no use for doctors.
____d. had forgotten to call the doctor.

Turn to the Comprehension Check on page 16 for the right answer.

Now read the story.
Read to find out who else stops by the Temples' home this Christmas Eve.

The Homecoming

The Judge had invited everyone back to his home. The Judge's main servant, Benjamin Pump, welcomed the Temples, the young hunter, and the others. Only a few candles burned as they entered. Other servants hurried to light more candles. Soon, the house was bright with light.

The Judge's cousin, Richard Jones, talked about the young hunter's accident. The young hunter stood in the hall. The others did not notice him. Finally Elizabeth said, "We forget, dear sirs, the strange young man. He came home with us to see the doctor."

"My shoulder wound is not serious," the young hunter said, entering the room. "I believe Judge Temple has sent for the doctor."

"Certainly," the Judge replied.

Richard Jones continued to talk to the Judge about the shooting accident. He offered to look at the wounded area himself.

"It will be well to wait for the doctor," the hunter said.

Jones replied angrily when the young man would not let him help. "The villagers think I don't know how to drive horses since you turned the sleigh." As he spoke, the village doctor, Elnathan Todd, arrived and was warmly welcomed by the Judge.

"Come in, come in," said the Judge, as the doctor entered the doorway. "Here is the young man I wounded by accident this evening."

The doctor took out an instrument. This tool would help take the bullet out of the young man's shoulder. When the young man saw the instrument, he began to tremble. "I believe, sir, that the bullet is only skin deep."

The doctor put the instrument down. He took out the bullet after he made a simple cut. When the doctor was done, there was a knock at the door. It was Indian John. He was also welcomed into the Temples' home.

Indian John stood at the end of the hall wrapped in his Indian blanket. His Mohegan tribe had lived in the area between the Hudson and the ocean. It had not been very long ago that he came to the mountains here.

Indian John and Leather-stocking were good friends. They both lived in the same kind of hut. They ate the same kinds of food, and often hunted together. Indian John called himself *Chingachgook*. The name means, 'Great Snake.' He called the wounded hunter *Young Eagle*.

Indian John told the Judge he should not have hurt Young Eagle. "Young Eagle has been struck by the hand that should do no wrong." He then used herbs for treatment of the wounded area. During Great Snake's treatment, talk turned to how much the Indians knew about herbs. When Great Snake had completed his treatment, the young hunter thought he should be going. But, first he asked about the deer that had been killed.

Those present wondered if the young hunter could have his share of the venison. The Judge ordered his servants to put the whole deer in a sleigh. "Take this young man to Leather-stocking's hut." Then he asked the young man his name.

"I am Oliver Edwards. I will return tomorrow for the sleigh."

The minister, Mr. Grant, said, "Forgive our wrongdoings as we forgive those who do wrong against us." The young man just smiled.

When young Oliver left, the minister told everyone he expected to see them in church later that evening. It will soon be Christmas. I trust I shall see you all at church." He looked at the Indian. "The man of the woods is important, too."

"John will come," said the Indian.

The church was a building used as a school, a church, and for other things. Ministers who passed through Templeton held their church meetings there. On Christmas Eve morning, Richard and one of his servants had entered the building. They had put up green tree branches in the church to make it look pretty for Christmas morning.

CTR 409-82

The Homecoming

COMPREHENSION CHECK

Preview Answer:
a. had sent for a doctor.

Choose the best answer.

1. The Judge's cousin is
____a. Young Eagle.
____b. Oliver Edwards.
____c. Richard Jones.
____d. Mr. Grant.

2. Richard Jones offers to
____a. take the young hunter home.
____b. look at Oliver's wound.
____c. treat Oliver's wound with herbs.
____d. take the bullet out of Oliver's shoulder.

3. Oliver Edwards
____a. is afraid he is going to die.
____b. knows he will get well.
____c. will never hunt again.
____d. does not like the doctor.

4. Who was the last person to arrive at the Judge's home?
____a. Elnathan Todd
____b. Mr. Grant
____c. Leather-stocking
____d. Indian John

5. Chingachgook treated Young Eagle's wound with
____a. the leaves and stems of plants.
____b. worms.
____c. ants.
____d. fresh berries.

6. Indian John thought the "accident"
____a. should have never happened.
____b. was a simple mistake.
____c. was planned.
____d. would teach everyone a lesson.

7. Oliver asked about the deer that had been killed. He wanted
____a. his share of the venison.
____b. the buck's fur.
____c. the buck's head.
____d. the whole buck.

8. When Oliver finally left,
____a. Elizabeth and her father went to church.
____b. the others sat down to dinner.
____c. the minister told everyone he expected to see them in church later that evening.
____d. Elizabeth wrapped Christmas gifts.

9. Another name for this story could be
____a. "Christmas in Templeton."
____b. "Young Eagle is Made Well."
____c. "Indian John's Visit."
____d. "Is There a Doctor in the House?"

10. This story is mainly about
____a. Oliver's wound being taken care of.
____b. Indian John and his herbs.
____c. why Indian John and Leather-stocking were good friends.
____d. why Richard Jones became angry with the young hunter.

Check your answers with the Key on page 67.

This page may be reproduced for classroom use.

The Homecoming

VOCABULARY CHECK

accident	area	hut	servant	shoulder	wound

I. Sentences to Finish
Fill in the blank in each sentence with the correct key word from the box above.

1. Joey had an ________with his bike yesterday; he rode right into a tree!
2. The __________ served his master well.
3. The boys built a _______ in the woods.
4. The deer's __________ was made by a hunter's arrow.
5. At the scene of the fire, the police told everyone to leave the _______ for their own safety.
6. When Rob tried to throw a fast ball, he hurt his ___________.

II. Matching
Write the letter of the correct meaning from Column B next to the key word in Column A.

Column A	Column B
____1. wound	a. a part of the body to which an arm is attached
____2. area	b. someone working in a house for pay
____3. accident	c. a hurt or injury caused by cutting, stabbing, etc.
____4. shoulder	d. something harmful that happens unexpectedly
____5. servant	e. a spot, space, or place
____6. hut	f. a small, roughly built house or dwelling

Check your answers with the Key on page 69.

This page may be reproduced for classroom use.

The Church Service

PREPARATION

Key Words

friendship (frend´ship) the condition of being friends
Carol and Joan's friendship has lasted many years.

future (fyü´ chər) the time to come; what is to come
The teacher said, "In the future, I expect you to hand in your work on time!"

God (god) an all-powerful being worshipped in most religions as the maker and ruler of the world
The poor woman often asked God for help.

guests (gests) people received in a home; visitors
Sheila invited some guests for dinner.

mistress (mis´ tris) a woman who is at the head of a household; a woman in charge of a home
Mrs. Ross is the mistress of the house.

pray (prā) talk to a higher being; ask help from God
Elsa asked the minister, "Will you pray for my sister? She's very sick."

The Church Service

Necessary Words

forbid (fər bid´) not allow someone to do something
The mother forbid her child to talk to the strange man.

fuel (fyü´ əl) anything that can be burned for heat or power
When we ran out of *fuel*, we had no heat in the house.

grace (grās) a prayer of thanks before or after a meal
Our family says grace before every meal.

service (sėr´ vis) a religious meeting
Church service begins every Sunday at ten o'clock.

Things

sugar-maple is a maple tree of eastern North America, valued for its hard wood and for its sweet sap, from which maple sugar and maple syrup are made. Judge Temple does not like to burn the sugar-maple as firewood.

CTR 409-83

The Church Service

As the guests wait to be called to dinner, the Judge talks with Richard.

Preview:
1. Read the name of the story.
2. Look at the picture.
3. Read the sentence under the picture.
4. Read the first two paragraphs of the story.
5. Then answer the following question.

You learned from your preview that Judge Temple

____a. burned coal for heat.
____b. forbid the use of any fuel.
____c. burned tree roots for fuel.
____d. did not like burning the sugar-maple.

Turn to the Comprehension Check on page 22 for the right answer.

Now read the story.
Read to find out who comes to the church service.

The Church Service

The Judge talked with Richard while they waited on the servant to call everyone to dinner. A large, sugar-maple log burned and warmed the room. The Judge showed his concern. "How often have I forbid the use of such wood in my house? Twenty years from now we shall want fuel. When the snow melts, we should send someone into the mountains and look for coal to use as fuel."

"Coal!" replied Richard. "We would kill more trees by digging up their roots to *look* for coal."

Richard then invited the Temples' guests to sit down for dinner. He asked the minister, Mr. Grant, to say grace. The minister said grace to thank God for their food.

When Elizabeth took her seat at the table, the Judge told everyone that she was now the 'mistress of my house.' He said, "As 'mistress of the house,' she should be called Miss Temple."

The other guests began talking about Indian John, Leather-stocking, and the young hunter. Some noted that even though the three appeared to have much in common, the young man was very well spoken.

Elizabeth's cheeks turned red when asked what she thought about him. Monsieur Le Quoi added his concern to the Judge's earlier one about the use of the trees. "We should forbid the killing of our trees."

Richard Jones' main servant said that he had seen the young hunter earlier. The Judge wondered how long the young man would be staying with Leather-stocking.

The Temples and their guests ate dinner. They enjoyed several kinds of meat, vegetables, and cakes. The bell from the school building rang. It announced that it was time for church.

The guests left in sleighs for the school building. Villagers along the way spoke to them as they rode by. Those who came from nearby towns placed blue and white blankets over their horses. The blankets kept the horses warm from the cold night.

Though Richard and his servant had added green tree branches inside of the building, the room was still quite plain. A large fire burning at each end of the room added a bright air.

All eyes turned to the door when Indian John, Leather-stocking, and the young hunter entered. The Indian took a seat next to the Judge. Leather-stocking sat on a log next to the fire and leaned his rifle against his leg. The young hunter sat on a bench with the other people.

Mr. Grant started the service. "God is in heaven; let all the earth keep silent before Him." The people stood. Elizabeth heard a young woman praying. "Dear God," she began, "we have not done those things we ought to have done."

When the minister's message was over, he began to pray for everyone. The people sat down on the benches until he finished his blessing. When the service was over, everyone wished each other a Merry Christmas.

Mr. Grant and his daughter Louisa came to where the Temples were sitting. Louisa and Elizabeth formed a quick friendship. They began planning things to do together. Mr. Grant warned that his daughter kept their house, and she didn't have too much free time for friendship.

After the Temples left, Indian John put out his hand to Mr. Grant. "I thank you. The words that you have spoken have gone up, and the Great Spirit is glad. I will tell my people the good talk I have heard."

Mr. Grant noted that Oliver Edwards seemed very comfortable in church. "I have attended church before," the young man explained.

The minister invited Edwards, Indian John, and Leather-stocking to go home with him and his daughter. "Oliver, my child has yet to thank you for saving my life earlier today." Then he told Leather-stocking he should think about his future. "You may have heard that young men *may* die, but old men *must*."

The old hunter still refused to join them. He said, "I must go to my hut. I don't worry about my future."

Indian John, Edwards, Mr. Grant and Louisa went down a path to the Grants' home. When they entered, they found a fire burning. It warmed the inside of the house. Louisa lighted some candles for light.

Mr. Grant talked with the young hunter about forgiveness. Their talk lasted for more than an hour before Edwards and Indian John left. Indian John took the short route to the village, while Edwards headed across the fields to the hut of Leather-stocking, beside the lake. Louisa stood at the window and watched until she could no longer see him.

CTR 409-83

The Church Service

COMPREHENSION CHECK

Preview Answer:
d. did not like burning the sugar-maple.

Choose the best answer.

1. Judge Temple would like to burn ________ for fuel, rather than trees.
    ____a. copper
    ____b. wheat
    ____c. coal
    ____d. leaves

2. Who, along with the Judge, thought the killing of trees should be forbidden?
    ____a. Richard Jones
    ____b. Elizabeth
    ____c. Mr. Grant
    ____d. Monsieur Le Quoi

3. When the guests sat down for dinner, who said grace?
    ____a. Judge Temple
    ____b. Mr. Grant
    ____c. Monsieur Le Quoi
    ____d. Elizabeth

4. When Elizabeth was asked what she thought about the young hunter, why do you think her cheeks turned red?
    ____a. She rather liked the young man.
    ____b. The fire was making her very warm.
    ____c. She was very, very cold.
    ____d. She had just finished a strong drink.

5. When the school bell rang, it was time
    ____a. to do the dishes.
    ____b. to ride the horses.
    ____c. to go to church.
    ____d. for mischief.

6. First, the Temples and their guests went to church. Then Indian John, Leather-stocking, and Oliver Edwards arrived at the church. Next,
    ____a. Louisa and Elizabeth formed a friendship.
    ____b. Mr. Grant talked to Leather-stocking about his future.
    ____c. Mr. Grant talked to Oliver about forgiveness.
    ____d. Mr. Grant started the service.

7. After the service, Indian John and Oliver Edwards
    ____a. went home with the Grants.
    ____b. went home with the Temples.
    ____c. went to Leather-stocking's hut.
    ____d. had a long talk about their friendship.

8. Louisa
    ____a. is a good housekeeper.
    ____b. has a great spirit.
    ____c. has no interest in young men.
    ____d. likes young Oliver.

9. Another name for this story could be
    ____a. "Burning the Sugar-Maple."
    ____b. "A Christmas Blessing."
    ____c. "School Bells Ringing."
    ____d. "No Time for Friendship."

10. This story is mainly about
    ____a. two young girls who have their eye on Oliver.
    ____b. Leather-stocking's future.
    ____c. how the people of Templeton shared Christmas.
    ____d. the Judge's concern about the killing of trees.

Check your answers with the Key on page 67.

This page may be reproduced for classroom use.

The Church Service

VOCABULARY CHECK

friendship	future	God	guests	mistress	pray

I. Sentences to Finish

Fill in the blank in each sentence with the correct key word from the box above.

1. After the accident, Pete thanked __________ for sparing his life.
2. Having much in common, Alice and Evelyn formed a lasting ____________.
3. Mother is the ____________of our house.
4. David wondered what his life would be like in the ___________.
5. How many ___________have you invited to the party?
6. In church, we __________ and sings songs to God.

II. Crossword Puzzle

Use the words from the box above to fill in the puzzle. Use the meanings below to help you choose the right answer.

Across

2. the time to come; what is to come
3. an all-powerful being who is worshipped
5. a woman who is the head of a household

Down

1. visitors
2. the condition of being friends
4. to talk to a higher being

1.
2.
3.
4.
5.

Check your answers with the Key on page 69.

This page may be reproduced for classroom use.

CTR 409-84

The Bold Dragoon Bar-room

PREPARATION

Key Words

action (ak´ shən) the process of acting; doing something
Lee took action to get the game started.

peace (pēs) order and quiet; without war or trouble
Europe welcomed peace after World War II came to an end.

purpose (pėr´ pəs) with a reason in mind; a plan; ***on purpose*** means "not by accident"; deliberately; intentionally
Mrs. Ross had a purpose for saving all her change. She wanted to buy her son a new bicycle for his birthday.

settle (set´ l) agree upon; bring to an end
"Let's settle our differences right here and now," said Joe.
The two girls wanted to settle their differences before they hurt their friendship.

sheriff (sher´ if) one who carries out the laws of a county; an officer of the law
The sheriff gave Mr. Allen a ticket for driving too fast.

turkey (tėr´ kē) a large bird used for food
The Martin family had turkey for Christmas dinner.

The Bold Dragoon Bar-room

Necessary Words

appoint	(ə point´)	to choose someone to do a job *The teacher will* *appoint* *a new team leader tomorrow.*
guilty	(gil´ tē)	having done wrong; found to have done wrong *John was found* *guilty* *of breaking the neighbor's window.*
lawyer	(lȯ´ yər) or (loi´ yər)	one who knows the laws and helps or gives advice to others about matters of law *Dan's* *lawyer* *worked hard to help Dan win the suit he brought against the town.*
responsibility	(ri spon´ sə bil´ ə tē)	one's duty or obligation to do something *Jason had a* *responsibility* *to feed his dogs every day.*
sermon	(sėr´ mən)	a talk or lesson given by a minister *The minister gave a* *sermon* *on helping those in need.*

People, Places, Things

Mr. and Mrs. Hollister are the owners of the Bold Dragoon Inn.

Justice of the Peace is a local magistrate (judge) who decides on local matters

The Bold Dragoon Bar-room

Mrs. Hollister welcomes her guests.

Preview:
1. Read the name of the story.
2. Look at the picture.
3. Read the sentence under the picture.
4. Read the first four paragraphs of the story.
5. Then answer the following question.

You learned from your preview that the lawyer in the Bold Dragoon thinks

____a. the Judge should pay for his crime.
____b. Oliver should forget about the accident.
____c. Oliver is looking for trouble.
____d. Oliver should take action against the doctor.

Turn to the Comprehension Check on page 28 for the right answer.

Now read the story.
Read to find out who the Judge appoints Sheriff of Templeton.

The Bold Dragoon Bar-room

In the very early hours of Christmas morning, the people of Templeton continued to gather together. Villagers met in the bar-room of the Bold Dragoon Inn. Fires burned to warm the room. Mrs. Hollister welcomed her guests. "I expect we'll be having the Judge, and the Major, and Mr. Jones down here soon," she said.

When Dr. Todd arrived, a lawyer who was in the Bold Dragoon bar-room spoke. "So, Dr. Todd, I hear you took a bullet out of the shoulder of Leather-stocking's son."

Dr. Todd looked puzzled. *This man is always talking foolish,* he thought. "I didn't know that Leather-stocking *had* a son," he answered.

The lawyer continued to talk about the accident. "I hope the young man is not going to let the matter drop. Do you think a man who owns as much land as the Judge has any more right to shoot a body than another?"

The doctor explained that the young hunter's wound was not serious.

The lawyer frowned. He spoke next to Hiram Doolittle, Justice of the Peace, who was seated next to the doctor. "I ask you, sir, if shooting a man on purpose is something that one could settle so easily?"

Hiram Doolittle gave the lawyer's question some thought. Finally he answered. "If a man is found guilty of shooting another on purpose, he could well be put away."

The lawyer smiled. He thought the Judge might pay the doctor for his treatment of the young hunter to settle the matter. Or perhaps the doctor could take action against the Judge if he were not willing to pay.

Before Dr. Todd had a chance to answer that he did not want to take action against the Judge, all eyes turned to the door. Leather-stocking had entered the bar-room. Talk continued about the responsibility of the Judge. Soon, the Judge and his guests arrived. Shortly after, Indian John walked in.

The villagers spoke to the Judge warmly. They shook his hand and wished him a Merry Christmas.

The Judge asked Mrs. Hollister how she liked Mr. Grant's sermon. She answered that she didn't think it was good that the minister *read* his sermon from the Book. "He should speak the sermon in his own words," she said, pouring him a drink.

The Judge talked to Leather-stocking. He talked about the new laws that were meant to keep peace between the villagers. "We now have the kinds of laws we need," he began. "One law forbids placing nets in our lakes and rivers out of season. Another law forbids the killing of deer and other animals except at certain times of the year. Now we just need a law that forbids the cutting down of trees in our woods!"

Leather-stocking told the Judge it would be hard to make people take on the responsibility of keeping these laws.

The Judge said that a good sheriff would see to it that the laws were followed.

The minutes turned into hours. Before long, the sun would be up. It was time for everyone to return home. The Hollister's were closing the bar-room.

It was a lovely Christmas morning. Elizabeth went outdoors. She thought she would take a nice walk. Her cousin Richard spotted her from his window. Opening the window he shouted, "Merry Christmas, cousin Bess! Wait for me, I'll be right down!"

Richard and Elizabeth took a walk toward the village. Richard asked his cousin if her father had any work for him. She held out a letter and said, "Why yes, he does, and it's an important office."

Richard read the letter from the Judge. I APPOINT RICHARD JONES SHERIFF OF TEMPLETON. Richard smiled. Then he said he would need to appoint others to help him. He would need help to make sure the villagers followed the laws, and to keep the peace in Templeton.

As they continued their walk, they heard some voices behind some bushes. Leather-stocking, Indian John, and the young hunter were talking.

Elizabeth wanted to leave so as not to hear what they were saying. But Richard, now the town's new sheriff, wanted to know what the men talked about.

"The bird must be had," said Leather-stocking, "by any means." He asked Indian John to shoot the bird. But, the Indian would not.

Elizabeth stepped out from behind the bushes so the men could see her. She offered to pay one of them to shoot her a Christmas turkey.

"Is this a thing for a lady?" asked Oliver.

Elizabeth handed Leather-stocking one dollar. He took the money and he and the others left.

Later, Elizabeth and Richard went to the place where young men gathered to shoot the Christmas turkey. They found Leather-stocking, Indian John, and the young hunter there.

The Bold Dragoon Bar-room

COMPREHENSION CHECK

Preview Answer:
a. the Judge should pay for his crime.

Choose the best answer.

1. The lawyer at the Bold Dragoon,
   ____a. had it in for the Judge.
   ____b. wanted the Judge's job.
   ____c. was looking for money.
   ____d. was just making small talk.

2. The lawyer believes that
   ____a. young Oliver's wound is serious.
   ____b. the shooting of young Oliver was no accident.
   ____c. Dr. Todd should not have helped young Oliver.
   ____d. men should not own guns.

3. The lawyer doesn't like the Judge because
   ____a. he owns land.
   ____b. he gets away with things because he's rich.
   ____c. he has no responsibilities.
   ____d. he has lots of money and owns a lot of land.

4. Hiram Doolittle is
   ____a. owner of the old Dragoon.
   ____b. Judge Temple's lawyer.
   ____c. Dr. Todd's brother.
   ____d. Justice of the Peace.

5. Leather-stocking thinks
   ____a. there are too many laws.
   ____b. there should be no laws.
   ____c. it will be hard to keep the new laws.
   ____d. no one should tell him what to do.

6. First Dr. Todd arrived at the bar-room. Then Leather-stocking arrived. Next entered,
   ____a. Judge Temple and his guests.
   ____b. Indian John.
   ____c. Oliver Edwards.
   ____d. Richard Jones.

7. Who did Judge Temple appoint Sheriff?
   ____a. Leather-stocking
   ____b. Richard Jones
   ____c. Mr. Grant
   ____d. Hiram Doolittle

8. The Judge appointed a sheriff to
   ____a. shoot the Christmas turkey.
   ____b. make sure that people followed the laws.
   ____c. keep law and order in the Bold Dragoon.
   ____d. raise money for a new church.

9. Another name for this story could be
   ____a. "Lawyer Talk."
   ____b. "No Peace in Templeton."
   ____c. "Richard Jones Becomes Sheriff."
   ____d. "The Christmas Turkey."

10. This story is mainly about
   ____a. neighbors who don't get along.
   ____b. the people of Templeton getting together to share the holiday spirit.
   ____c. a lawyer who wants to make trouble for the Judge.
   ____d. shooting the Christmas turkey.

Check your answers with the Key on page 67.

This page may be reproduced for classroom use.

The Bold Dragoon Bar-room

VOCABULARY CHECK

action	peace	purpose	settle	sheriff	turkey

I. Sentences to Finish

Fill in the blank in each sentence with the correct key word from the box above.

1. The quick ________ of the firemen saved the children in the burning house.
2. Some families like lamb for Christmas dinner. Our family likes ____________.
3. Pat and Kim tried to __________ on a time to meet for lunch.
4. The __________ took the thief to jail.
5. Ann had a __________ for studying so hard. She wanted the best grade on the test!
6. In the city, I found very little __________, so I moved to the country where it's quiet.

II. Word Search

All the words in the box above are hidden in the puzzle below. They may be written from left to right, up and down, or on an angle. As you find each word, put a circle around it.

T	P	E	A	L	A	C	T	S
U	P	A	C	T	I	O	N	H
R	E	U	S	E	T	T	L	E
K	A	I	R	F	F	P	L	R
A	C	T	T	P	F	U	E	I
L	E	P	U	R	O	R	C	F
T	U	R	K	E	Y	S	P	F
P	S	H	E	R	F	F	E	P

Check your answers with the Key on page 70.

This page may be reproduced for classroom use.

CTR 409-85

The Judge's Assistant

PREPARATION

Key Words

claim	(klām)	demand as your own right; to make something your own *If the ring's owner can't be found, Jean will claim the ring as her own, as she found it.*
reminded	(ri mīnd′ əd)	to have made a person think or remember something; caused to remember *The teacher reminded the class that there would be a test tomorrow.*
skill	(skil)	an ability gained by knowledge and practice *John shows great skill with a bow and arrow.*
spent	(spent)	used up *Jane spent all her money on candy.* *Karen spent many hours studying for the test.*
sugar	(shu̇g′ ər)	a sweet substance widely used in food products *The cake called for two cups of sugar.* *Mother baked sugar cookies today.*
suggested	(sə jest′ əd)	put forward an idea; proposed *When Trevor suggested we play football, we all said, "yes."*

The Judge's Assistant

Necessary Words

annual	(an´ yü əl)	once a year *Christmas is an annual event.*
assistant	(ə sis´ tənt)	one who helps another *Cindy is the teacher's new assistant.*
click	(klik)	a short, sharp sound *I heard a click as the dime went down the coin slot.*
sap	(sap)	a liquid found in plants and trees *Maple syrup is made from the sap of the sugar-maple tree.*

CTR 409-85

The Judge's Assistant

At the annual Christmas Turkey Shoot, Billy Kirby takes aim.

Preview:
1. Read the name of the story.
2. Look at the picture.
3. Read the sentence under the picture.
4. Read the first seven paragraphs of the story.
5. Then answer the following question.

You learned from your preview that __________owned the birds.

____a. a free, black man
____b. Billy Kirby
____c. Natty Bumppo
____d. Richard Jones

Turn to the Comprehension Check on page 34 for the right answer.

Now read the story.
Read to find out who will become the Judge's new assistant.

The Judge's Assistant

Twenty or thirty young men with rifles met for the annual Christmas Turkey Shoot. Many of the boys in the village stood around the hunters. The boys listened to the hunters boast about their hunting skills. The chief speaker of the group was Billy Kirby. He was a man in Templeton who cleared land and chopped wood. Kirby and Leather-stocking had many contests over who had the best skill with a rifle.

A free, black man owned the birds. He charged one dollar for one shot. The Black gave the rule that the bird must be shot in an area of feathers for the shooter to claim the bird.

Billy Kirby announced he would shoot first. "Stand out of the way there, boys, or I will shoot right through you!"

"Stop!" cried the young hunter who had just arrived. "I am here to shoot, too. Here is my dollar."

Billy Kirby reminded the young hunter that he had a shoulder wound. "It will take a good shot to hit that bird."

Leather-stocking placed his rifle in the snow and leaned on the barrel. "Don't be boasting, Billy Kirby," he suggested.

The wood chopper took careful aim with his rifle and fired at the bird. When the shot missed, the Black offered him a second chance.

"No - the shot is mine," said the young hunter.

Like Billy Kirby, Leather-stocking reminded the young hunter of his shoulder wound. He offered to take the shot for him.

"The chance is mine," said the young hunter. He took aim, fired, and missed the bird, too.

Now Leather-stocking took his chance, but instead of a shot from the rifle, there was only a click.

The Black said, "A click's as good as fire. Natty Bumppo miss a turkey!"

Talk followed on if a click should be called a shot. Elizabeth settled it. She said that Leather-stocking would need to pay another dollar for another shot.

Billy Kirby shot again and missed. The young hunter said that his shoulder would stop him from trying again. Leather-stocking then aimed and hit the turkey. He claimed the bird, and gave it to Elizabeth. She gave it to the young hunter. "Please, sir, take this bird as a small offering for the hurt that kept you from your own shot."

The Shoot continued, and the Judge arrived. He called the young hunter to him and suggested, "Become my assistant for a season. I will pay you well."

When the young hunter refused the offer, Leather-stocking reminded the Judge there was a good life to be had living in the forest. After talking some more about the offer, the young hunter took the job as the Judge's assistant.

After the Judge, Elizabeth, and Richard left the Shoot, they talked about the young hunter's new work.

As the young hunter, Leather-stocking, and Mohegan left the annual Turkey Shoot, they, too, spoke of the new job. The young hunter stopped their talk. "Enough is said, my friends! I feel I must do it."

The day ended with another service led by Mr. Grant. The close of Christmas Day, 1793, ended on a warm note. Heavy rains melted the snow, and the dark pines could be easily seen. Elizabeth and Louisa Grant enjoyed the evening together in the Temples' home. While her father was away from Templeton, Louisa spent lots of time in the Temples' home. Oliver Edwards began his work for the Judge, but spent most of his nights with Leather-stocking.

Spring came. The snow melted, and the scene in Templeton changed. One day, Richard, Edwards, the Judge, Elizabeth, and Louisa stopped by to pick up Monsieur Le Quoi at his home. They all rode their horses up in the hills. As they rode, they spoke of the lovely weather. They soon reached Billy Kirby's camp. They found him boiling sap to make maple sugar. The Judge frowned. He was not pleased.

"I'll turn my back to no man in these hills for boiling down the sugar-maple sap," said Billy. He then went on to explain the skill of sugar-making.

The Judge looked at the area and was concerned about the way Kirby had been making cuts in the trunks of the sugar-maples. "Kirby, you make big wounds in these trees where a small cut would work."

After Kirby told the Judge there were more than enough trees in the area, the riding party descended the mountain to return to Templeton.

CTR 409-85

The Judge's Assistant

COMPREHENSION CHECK

Preview Answer:

a. a free, black man

Choose the best answer.

1. The hunters at the Turkey Shoot boasted about
   ____a. their hunting skills.
   ____b. their courage.
   ____c. their fears.
   ____d. the gifts they received for Christmas.

2. At the Turkey Shoot, who fired his rifle first?
   ____a. Natty Bumppo
   ____b. The young hunter
   ____c. Judge Temple
   ____d. Billy Kirby

3. First the wood chopper fired at a turkey and missed. Then the black man offered him a second chance. Next,
   ____a. Leatherstocking shot a turkey.
   ____b. the young hunter fired, but missed the bird.
   ____c. Elizabeth gave a turkey to the young hunter.
   ____d. the Judge offered the young hunter a job.

4. The cost to take a shot at a bird was
   ____a. twenty-five cents.
   ____b. fifty cents.
   ____c. one dollar.
   ____d. a nickel.

5. Who was the first to claim a turkey?
   ____a. The young hunter
   ____b. Judge Temple
   ____c. Billy Kirby
   ____d. Leather-stocking

6. The Judge *probably* offered the young hunter a job because
   ____a. he needed someone strong to assist him around the house.
   ____b. the wounded young man could not earn a living.
   ____c. he felt he owed him something in return for shooting him.
   ____d. Elizabeth had asked him to.

7. At the end of the day,
   ____a. more snow had fallen.
   ____b. it rained very hard.
   ____c. the wind picked up.
   ____d. the sun came out.

8. Judge Temple was concerned with the way
   ____a. Billy Kirby boiled sap.
   ____b. Billy Kirby set up camp.
   ____c. Billy Kirby spoke to him.
   ____d. Billy made cuts in the trunks of sugar-maples.

9. Another name for this story could be
   ____a. "At the Annual Christmas Turkey Shoot."
   ____b. "Turkey Feathers."
   ____c. "The Young Hunter Looks for a Job."
   ____d. "Spring Arrives at Last."

10. This story is mainly about
    ____a. why Leather-stocking's rifle did not fire.
    ____b. who took home the Christmas turkey.
    ____c. how some people in Templeton spent Christmas Day.
    ____d. the skill of sugar-making.

Check your answers with the Key on page 67.

This page may be reproduced for classroom use.

The Judge's Assistant

VOCABULARY CHECK

claim	reminded	skill	spent	sugar	suggested

I. Sentences to Finish
Fill in the blank in each sentence with the correct key word from the box above.

1. I wonder if anyone will _________ the money I found.

2. Dad puts too much _________ in his coffee. It's much too sweet.

3. Theresa _________ a lot of time helping those in need.

4. Dad _________Mother that he had invited some friends over this evening.

5. "I took the short-cut as you __________," said Paul, "but I got lost!"

6. Keith shows great _________ on the basketball court.

II. Using the Words - On the lines below, write six of your own sentences using the key words from the box above. Use each word once, and circle the key word.

1. ____

2. ____

3. ____

4. ____

5. ____

6. ____

Check your answers with the Key on page 70.

This page may be reproduced for classroom use.

Spring in the Village

PREPARATION

Key Words

accept	(ak sept´)	to take what is offered *"I will accept your excuse for arriving late," said the teacher.* *I will accept Jill's offer to help me with my homework.*
agree/agreed	(ə grē´) (ə grēd´)	1. to have the same feeling or opinion as someone else *Larry and Wanda can't agree on anything!* 2. consented *Tim agreed to meet me for breakfast.*
pigeons	(pij´ ənz)	birds with thick bodies and short tails and legs *Six pigeons are sitting on the fence.*
pride/prided	(prīd) (prīd´ əd)	a good feeling one has about one's own worth; having had a good feeling about one's own worth *Jim takes pride in his work.* *Alex prided himself on his pitching skills.*
rough	(ruf)	not smooth; not level; not even *We had a rough ride on the roller-coaster.* *The bark on the old oak tree is very rough.*
spear	(spir)	a weapon with a long shaft and a pointed end *The end of the spear was very sharp.*

Spring in the Village

Necessary Words

bass (bas) a fish related to the sunfish
Jim caught two bass at the lake.

bridle (brī´ dl) the part of a horse's harness that fits around the horse's head
Mary needed help putting the bridle on her horse.

challenge/challenged
(chal´ ənj) call to a contest
(chal´ ənjd) *John will challenge Mark to a game of rummy.*
Jeff challenged Tim to a race on foot.

recover/recovered get back to a normal condition
(ri kuv´ ər) *It took Edna three weeks to recover from her cold.*
(ri kuv´ ərd) got back to a normal condition
Gregory has not fully recovered from the accident.

thrown (thrōn) the past of *throw*; sent through the air; tossed
"I should have thrown the ball to third base!" cried Ron.

Places

Pennsylvania a middle Atlantic state of the U.S.A.

CTR 409-86

Spring in the Village

When a tree cracks and begins to fall, Edward reaches out to help Louisa, while the Judge reaches out for his daughter.

Preview:
1. Read the name of the story.
2. Look at the picture.
3. Read the sentence under the picture.
4. Read the first eight paragraphs of the story.
5. Then answer the following question.

You learned from your preview that years ago, Judge Temple

____a. bought food for the people in Templeton.
____b. lived in Europe.
____c. lived in Pennsylvania.
____d. sold food at high prices.

Turn to the Comprehension Check on page 40 for the right answer.

Now read the story.
Read to find out how Leather-stocking is different from the men living in the village.

Spring in the Village

Leaving Kirby's camp, the group descended the mountain. Richard and his horse led the way down. The trail was rough. The Judge kept an eye on Elizabeth. He watched to make sure her horse didn't fall. "Easy, easy my child," he suggested, as she rode over a rough pass.

The Judge explained to the riding party about how life used to be here. "There once was a time when food was scarce here. Food got a high price in Europe."

Elizabeth asked her father what he did to help those who were hungry.

"I bought wheat from Pennsylvania for the people in Templeton. We made nets and dragged the lake for fish." He held his arm out and said, "Once there was nothing here but the lake, mountain and forests. One day I saw smoke curling from a hut near the mountain."

"It was the hut of Leather-stocking," Edwards said.

"It was," the Judge replied. "He invited me over to spend the night. I slept on a bear skin."

Suddenly, a large crack was heard and Edwards shouted, "A tree! A tree! Run for your lives!" He reached for the bridle of Louisa's horse.

The Judge grabbed the bridle of his daughter's horse and pulled him forward. "God save my child!" he shouted.

A large tree then fell across their path. It missed all of them. Louisa was scared by the near miss. She had to be helped by Edwards and Elizabeth. After she recovered, they continued on down the path. Before they reached the village, it began to snow. A large storm soon took away all signs of spring.

At the end of April the snow finally disappeared. One day Richard asked Elizabeth to a pigeon hunt. She, Louisa, and the Judge joined Richard for the event. Many others came with their rifles. Leather-stocking came too, his rifle ready. He told Billy Kirby that firing into so many pigeons was not right. Kirby challenged Leather-stocking to a contest to kill just *one* bird. Leather-stocking agreed to the challenge. He picked up his rifle, took aim at a pigeon, and the dead bird fell to the ground.

"What!" said young Edwards. "Have you really killed a bird on the wing, Natty, with a single ball?"

"Yes," said Leather-stocking. He then spoke of the waste of killing so many birds. The Judge agreed with him. Leather-stocking then left and disappeared into the bushes around the lake.

Later in the spring the villagers began bass fishing in the lake. Richard invited Elizabeth to watch him fish. Elizabeth, Louisa, Edwards, and the Judge joined Richard. They sat around a fire on the banks of the lake while Richard fished for bass.

Richard, Billy Kirby, and the Judge's main servant, Benjamin Pump, were in one boat. Benjamin prided himself in his skill to throw the net. Once the net was thrown, they pulled it to shore. It was filled with many fish. The Judge said that it was a waste to catch so many fish. "One day the fish will disappear just like the sugar-maples."

While the men divided the catch, Elizabeth and Louisa took a walk along the bank of the lake. Elizabeth saw a fire on the other side of the lake. She thought it was at the hut of Leather-stocking. She and Louisa talked about what was known about him. "He does not like our ways," said Elizabeth.

Soon Leather-stocking and Mohegan arrived at their side of the lake in a small boat. Leather-stocking carried a fishing spear. The Judge asked if he would accept some of the evening's catch.

"No, no," the old hunter replied. He would not accept the fish. "I eat of no man's wasty ways. I use my spear to catch the fish I will eat."

"We agree on that, old hunter," said the Judge.

Elizabeth asked if she could ride in their boat. Mohegan agreed to give her and Louisa a safe ride. Edwards jumped on board, too.

During their ride, Natty caught a large fish with his spear. The men in the other boat continued pulling fish in with the net they had thrown. Then, Benjamin fell out of the boat. Not knowing how to swim, he began to sink. Leather-stocking quickly used his spear to pull him out of the water. Benjamin quickly recovered, but his pride was wounded.

Later that evening they all returned to the village. Elizabeth wondered what it would be like to visit the hut of Leather-stocking. One day she would find out.

CTR 409-86

Spring in the Village

COMPREHENSION CHECK

Preview Answer:
a. bought food for the people in Templeton.

Choose the best answer.

1. Judge Temple remembers a time in Templeton when
   ____a. life was easy.
   ____b. food was not easy to come by.
   ____c. horses were scarce.
   ____d. it was against the law to fish in the lake.

2. When the people of Templeton had fallen on hard times,
   ____a. they planted more vegetables in their gardens.
   ____b. they hunted bear for food.
   ____c. they went fishing in Pennsylvania.
   ____d. the Judge bought wheat to feed the hungry.

3. As Richard and the others descended the mountain,
   ____a. they lost their way.
   ____b. a bear began to chase them.
   ____c. a fire broke out in the forest.
   ____d. a tree snapped and fell across their path.

4. Before Richard and his group reached home,
   ____a. it began to snow.
   ____b. it started to rain.
   ____c. they found themselves in the middle of an ice storm.
   ____d. the sun came out.

5. Leather-stocking and Judge Temple believe that
   ____a. it's wrong to take more than you need of anything.
   ____b. there's plenty of everything to go around.
   ____c. it's wrong to kill pigeons.
   ____d. young ladies belong at home.

6. Richard and the others are fishing for
   ____a. bait.
   ____b. bones.
   ____c. bass.
   ____d. blues.

7. The ways of Leather-stocking and Mohegan
   ____a. frighten Elizabeth.
   ____b. are different than the ways of the villagers.
   ____c. are not welcome in Templeton.
   ____d. are not respected by the villagers.

8. First, the men in Richard's boat pulled in their catch. Then, Ben Pump fell out of the boat. Next,
   ____a. Ben used his skill to throw the net.
   ____b. Leather-stocking pulled Ben out of the water.
   ____c. Ben Pump began to drown.
   ____d. Ben Pump recovered.

9. Another name for this story could be
   ____a. "Something's Fishy."
   ____b. "The Pigeon Hunt."
   ____c. "Springtime Adventures."
   ____d. "Kirby's Challenge."

10. This story is mainly about
   ____a. learning how to fish and hunt.
   ____b. how Benjamin Pump almost drowned.
   ____c. what happened to Richard and his group as they traveled down the mountain.
   ____d. how some villagers spend their time when winter is over and the warm weather arrives.

Check your answers with the Key on page 67.

This page may be reproduced for classroom use.

Spring in the Village

VOCABULARY CHECK

accept	agree/agreed	pigeons	pride/prided	rough	spear

I. Sentences to Finish
Fill in the blank in each sentence with the correct key word from the box above.

1. Sally's hands are very __________. She should wear gloves when washing dishes.
2. The old man living in the forest hunts animals with a __________.
3. Everyday I go to the park to feed the __________.
4. "Please _________ my gift along with my deepest thanks."
5. Jill takes ___________ in being a good baby-sitter.
6. Samantha _____________ not to share my secret with anyone.

II. Making Sense of Sentences
Put a check next to YES if the sentence makes sense. Put a check next to NO if the sentence does not make sense.

1. Dad and Mother ***agree*** that I'm too young to drive. ___YES ___NO
2. Donna wore a green ***spear*** to the party. ___YES ___NO
3. George will not ***accept*** help from anyone. ___YES ___NO
4. When Tom lost his key, he ***pride*** the door open. ___YES ___NO
5. We saw many ***pigeons*** at the park. ___YES ___NO
6. Martha's ***rough*** hands are very soft. ___YES ___NO

Check your answers with the Key on page 70.

This page may be reproduced for classroom use.

CTR 409-87

Breaking the Law

PREPARATION

Key Words

August (ȯ gust´) the eighth month of the year
John's school year begins on August 8th.

greet (grēt) to welcome; say 'hello' to
greeted (grēt´ əd) to have welcomed; to have said 'hello' to
Ben went to the door to greet his Aunt Rose.
"Alice, have you greeted all the guests?" asked Mark.

January (jan´ yü er´ ē) the first month of the year
New Year's Day is January 1st.

leap (lēp) to jump
leaped (lēpt) to have jumped
Max was ready to leap off the diving board and into the pool.
Beth leaped into the pool first.

protection (prə tek´ shən) safety
Sue's family bought a dog for their protection.

sight (sīt) view
Mary tried to find her lost kitten, but it was nowhere in sight.

Breaking the Law

Necessary Words

justice (jus´ tis) just treatment; deserved reward or punishment

Justice demands that all people be treated the same in a court of law.

leash (lēsh) a strap or chain for holding an animal in check

Jamie fastened the leash to his dog's collar, then took him for a walk.

panther (pan´ thər) a mountain lion; a black leopard

"Don't get too close to the panther's cage," said the zookeeper to the little boy and his mother.

perch (pėrch) a small fish found in the fresh waters of North America

Dad and Junior caught eight perch today. Mom says we're having perch for dinner.

CTR 409-87

Breaking the Law

A young panther attacks Brave.

Preview:
1. Read the name of the story.
2. Look at the picture.
3. Read the sentence under the picture.
4. Read the first five paragraphs of the story.
5. Then answer the following question.

You learned from your preview that Oliver Edwards had been living with the Temples for

____a. a few days.
____b. a few weeks.
____c. several months.
____d. more than one year.

Turn to the Comprehension Check on page 46 for the right answer.

Now read the story.
Read to find out what happens when Elizabeth and Louisa go for a walk.

Breaking the Law

When Richard saw the Judge the next day, he found his cousin had not slept well. The Judge showed him the letter that had kept him awake all night. It appeared that the Judge might have to leave Templeton for a time.

Elizabeth and Louisa decided to take a walk on the mountain path. The Judge was concerned. He said, "Stray not too deep into the forest. There are hidden dangers there."

"Not at this season," said Elizabeth.

Oliver Edwards was heading to the lake to fish. He had heard the Judge and Elizabeth talking, for he had been staying with the Temples for several months. He caught up to the girls. "Your father is not pleased that you should walk without help in these hills, Miss Temple. If I might offer myself for your protection. . ."

"I thank you, Mr. Edwards, but if I need help, I will bring Brave." She called her dog, Brave, to her side. "It would be best if you would catch some perch for dinner."

As they continued on their walk, Edwards went to the lake and took one of the Judge's small boats. He rowed across the lake to the hut of Leather-stocking. Natty's dogs greeted him. After spending about an hour in the hut, he joined Natty and Mohegan on the lake to fish.

The men then sat silently while they fished for perch. Suddenly, a buck ran through the woods and jumped into the lake, Natty's dogs giving chase until they reached water. When the buck neared their boats, Natty stood with his rifle to shoot it.

"Hold!" exclaimed Edwards, "remember the law, my old friend. You are in plain sight of the village. I know that Judge Temple will bring all who kill deer out of season to justice. Just hold your hand, Natty. I'll rescue the buck."

As Edwards' boat neared the buck, he threw a rope around him. Just as he did, Natty's boat came close. The old hunter cut the throat of the animal, and drew the dead buck into the boat.

"So much for Judge Temple's law!" said Leather-stocking. "This will be good venison."

The men rowed their boats to shore to see who had let the dogs loose. Natty saw that a knife had been used to cut the dogs' leather leashes.

Elizabeth and Louisa continued their walk in the woods. Their path took them to a place on the mountain above Leather-stocking's hut. When they neared the top of the mountain, Brave came to Elizabeth's side. He caught sight of something moving in the woods above them.

Elizabeth glanced up in the same direction and saw a young panther ready to leap.

"Let us fly!" Elizabeth said, taking Louisa's arm. "Courage, Brave! Courage!"

Suddenly, the young panther attacked the dog. Brave sent the animal flying. A larger panther then leaped and killed Brave, even with his fierce fight.

"Get lower, girl!" a voice called out. "Your hat hides the panther's head!"

When Elizabeth lowered her head, a bullet flew by and hit the panther. Natty moved closer to the wounded animal and shot him again in the head.

"Come. . .come," Leather-stocking said to the frightened young ladies. "Let us get to the road. You've had enough scare to make you wish to be in your father's house again."

For their protection, Natty walked with them a little way. He watched as they began to descend the mountain path. When he returned to the forest, he ran into Squire Hiram Doolittle.

"How goes it, Natty?" asked Mr. Doolittle, stepping out of the bushes to greet the old hunter. When he saw Natty's rifle, he added, "What! Shooting this warm day? Mind, old man, the law don't get hold of you."

"What has a man who lives in the forests to do with the ways of the law?" asked Leather-stocking.

"I suppose you know there is a fine for any man who kills a deer between January and August."

"And how much goes to the man who tells someone this happened between January and August?" asked Natty.

"He gets half," the Squire said. He then saw the blood on the old hunter's clothes.

Natty pointed to the dead panther in the bushes. He said that there was no law against killing panthers.

Natty took the Squire's knife and cut a piece of leather on his dog's leash. He said, "I think this knife has cut leather before."

Doolittle asked, "Are you saying that I let your dogs loose?" He continued, "I know you broke the law. I will see that you receive justice before you are one day older."

Natty pointed his finger at the Justice of the Peace. "Away with you! If I ever catch your sorry face in the woods again, take care that I don't mistake you for an owl!"

Hiram Doolittle hurried away.

CTR 409-87

Breaking the Law

COMPREHENSION CHECK

Preview Answer:
c. several months.

Choose the best answer.

1. The letter that Judge Temple received,
   ____a. troubled him.
   ____b. excited him.
   ____c. interested him.
   ____d. clouded his thinking.

2. Oliver Edwards offered the girls his
   ____a. company.
   ____b. wisdom.
   ____c. bait.
   ____d. protection.

3. Who went fishing to catch some perch?
   ____a. Leather-stocking
   ____b. Mohegan
   ____c. Oliver Edwards
   ____d. All of the above (a,b,c)

4. A buck ran through the woods and into the lake, followed by
   ____a. Judge Temple.
   ____b. Billy Kirby and his rifle.
   ____c. a pack of barking dogs.
   ____d. other deer.

5. First, Natty stood in his boat and raised his rifle at the buck. Then Edwards warned him of the law. Next,
   ____a. Natty took aim and shot the buck.
   ____b. Edwards rescued the buck.
   ____c. Edwards threw a rope around the buck.
   ____d. Leather-stocking cut the buck's throat.

6. Leatherstocking feels
   ____a. that deer should not be hunted out of season.
   ____b. that people should be allowed to hunt all year.
   ____c. a great respect for the law.
   ____d. deer should not be hunted.

7. Brave was killed by
   ____a. a bullet.
   ____b. an arrow.
   ____c. a buck.
   ____d. a panther.

8. Who cut Natty's dogs loose?
   ____a. Hiram Doolittle
   ____b. Mohegan
   ____c. Judge Temple
   ____d. Richard Jones

9. Another name for this story could be
   ____a. "Natty Saves the Day."
   ____b. "Going Fishing."
   ____c. "A Dog's Courage."
   ____d. "Killing Deer Out of Season."

10. This story is mainly about
    ____a. why Natty broke the law.
    ____b. a man who grew up in the forest and refuses to change his ways.
    ____c. how Natty saved the lives of Elizabeth and Louisa.
    ____d. a dog who died trying to save his master.

Check your answers with the Key on page 67.

This page may be reproduced for classroom use.

Breaking the Law

VOCABULARY CHECK

August	greet/greeted	January	leap/leaped	protection	sight

I. Sentences to Finish
Fill in the blank in each sentence with the correct key word from the box above.

1. With no land in _____________, Robbie was afraid he and his boat might never be found.
2. The men _______________ each other with a firm handshake.
3. For my own _______________, I wear a helmet when riding a bike.
4. My birthday is July 4th. My sister's birthday is next month, _____________ 2nd.
5. The day after December 31st is _________________ 1st.
6. The thief _______________ over the wall to make his getaway.

II. Matching
Write the letter of the correct meaning from Column B next to the key word in Column A.

Column A	Column B
____1. protection	a. view
____2. greet	b. the first month of the year
____3. August	c. to welcome; to say hello to
____4. leap	d. the eighth month of the year
____5. sight	e. to jump
____6. January	f. safety

Check your answers with the Key on page 71.

This page may be reproduced for classroom use.

The Arrest

PREPARATION

Key Words

arrest	(a rest´)	to take into custody (in the care of police) *The police went to the thief's home and placed him under arrest.*
court	(kôrt)	a place where justice is served by a judge or jury (people chosen to decide if one is guilty or not) *The court found the man to be guilty as charged.*
information	(in´ fər mā´ shən)	knowledge; facts *If anyone has information about the robbery, please call the police.*
officer	(ȯ´ fə sər)	one who holds a public, government, or other office, like a police officer *The police officer gave the driver a speeding ticket.*
person	(per´ sən)	a man, woman, or child; a human being *Any person who wishes may come to my party.* *Shelly is a lovely person.*
prison	(priz´ n)	a place where people are held against their will; a place where lawbreakers are sent *The man who killed his brother went to prison for forty years.*

The Arrest

Necessary Words

document (dok´ yə mənt) a piece of paper that gives information or proves a fact
The document proved that the boy was old enough to drive.

miner (mī´ nər) one who works in a mine (a place under the earth where we find things like gold, coal, salt, gems, etc.)
The miner came home every day covered in coal dust.

mining (mī´ ning) the act of digging under the earth for coal or other minerals (things found under the earth that are neither plant nor animal)
The men were mining for gold.

native (nā´ tiv) a person is *native* to the place where he was born
Jason is a native of New York.

offense (ə fəns´) something that is done against the law; a crime
Since this was Harry's first offense, the judge went easy on him.
Joel's offense was running a red light.

ore (ôr) rocks, sand, or dirt containing minerals like gold, silver, etc.
Gold ore was discovered in California in the mid 1800's.

CTR 409-88

The Arrest

Richard and the Judge ride their horses up the mountain.

Preview:

1. Read the name of the story.
2. Look at the picture.
3. Read the sentence under the picture.
4. Read the first five paragraphs of the story.
5. Then answer the following question.

You learned from your preview that Richard thinks

____a. Natty has been mining for gold on the Judge's land.
____b. Squire Doolittle's information cannot be trusted.
____c. that Oliver Edwards isn't who he says he is.
____d. that the Judge is too easy on the natives.

Turn to the Comprehension Check on page 52 for the right answer.

Now read the story.

Read to find out what happens when court officers arrive at Leather-stocking's hut.

The Arrest

Richard and the Judge rode their horses up the mountain. Richard asked the Judge, "What do you think about Natty, Mohegan, and Edwards being together?"

"I was just thinking on that," replied the Judge.

His cousin went on. "You know there are mines in these mountains. The natives have long known that gold can be found here. I think that natives like Leather-stocking and Mohegan know of such mines. They have been seen going up and coming down from the mountain with mining tools. Others have seen them carrying things into their hut. While they grow rich with their mining, you grow poor. And do you know who this Oliver Edwards really is?"

The Judge did not answer the question about Edwards. But he was curious about Richard's other information. Would Natty be mining on his land? "How much of this is made up in your head, and how much have you really heard from others?"

"I got my information from Squire Doolittle. He saw Natty on the mountain and offered to help him carry his load. But Natty refused to let him help."

The Judge explained that Edwards was too poor a person to have any gold.

"Well, it would be a *poor* person who would need it!" exclaimed Richard.

The Judge had forgotten why they had gone up the mountain. "Why are we here?" he asked his cousin.

Richard explained that a miner named Jotham had shown him a place where there was ore. It was an area near Leather-stocking's hut. They rode to the spot and found the miner digging in a hole. The Judge got off his horse. Richard showed him mining tools that were hidden in the bushes, suggesting that they belonged to Natty, Mohegan, and Edwards.

The Judge searched the hole, but he didn't find ore. Just then, he saw Elizabeth and Louisa coming toward him. They told him of their scare with the panther, and how Natty had killed it. The Judge had only kind thoughts for the person who had saved his child.

Back at home, Elizabeth was going over the day's events with her father, when the Squire stopped by. He told the Judge that Natty had killed a deer. "He has the deer's skin in his hut! I need a court document that will allow me to search Natty's hut."

The Judge did not want to make trouble for Natty. But, the law was the law. He gave the Squire the document.

Sheriff Jones could not be found, so the Squire took Billy Kirby and Jotham with him to Leather-stocking's. They would be acting as court officers. On the way to Natty's, the Squire said, "The Judge is set on putting the deer law into force. Someone has killed a deer out of season."

"Who?" asked Billy.

"You will see," replied Doolittle.

When they neared Leather-stocking's hut, Billy's heart skipped a beat. "Not *Natty!*" he cried. "Why, he was *born* on this mountain. This person should not be forced to follow this silly law!"

When the officers arrived at the hut, Leather-stocking refused to let them in.

"I have a court document that allows me to search your place," said the Squire.

At those words, Natty raised his rifle and took aim at the officers, sending Doolittle and the miner down the mountain.

Billy laughed. Then he asked Natty to give himself up.

Natty said, "No. I have the buck, and I will pay the fine. But you will not arrest me!"

Sometime later, Edwards learned from Mr. Lippett, a village lawyer, about Natty's offense. The lawyer explained that killing a buck out of season was a small offense, but pointing a rifle at a court officer was a serious one. Natty could go to prison for such an offense.

"Prison!" replied Edwards. "No, no. That would *kill* the old man!"

Edwards ran to Judge Temple's. He told him what the lawyer had said.

"I'm sorry," said the Judge sadly, "but the law is the law. Natty pointed a rifle at court officers."

Edwards began shouting. "But this is not *right!* Look into your heart, if you have one, and right this wrong!"

"Oliver!" shouted Marmaduke. "Have you forgotten who you're talking to? I have heard, young man, that you are mining on my land. I think it is best if we part ways." So Edwards left the Temples' home.

That night, the Sheriff was sent to Natty's hut to place him under arrest. When he and his men got to the hut, they found it had been burned. The old hunter came out of the woods. "What would you do with an old and helpless man?" he asked.

Natty was arrested.

CTR 409-88

The Arrest

COMPREHENSION CHECK

Preview Answer:
a. Natty has been mining for gold on the Judge's land.

Choose the best answer.

1. Richard believes that
   ____a. the Judge should buy some mining tools.
   ____b. the natives are stealing gold from the Judge's land.
   ____c. the natives are poor.
   ____d. Judge Temple is becoming poor.

2. After listening to Richard, Judge Temple asks him
   ____a. to find out more about the natives.
   ____b. to show him the mines.
   ____c. to stop poking around his land.
   ____d. if his information is correct.

3. Where did Richard get his information?
   ____a. Squire Doolittle
   ____b. Jotham
   ____c. Billy Kirby
   ____d. Louisa

4. Richard took the Judge to an area near Leather-stocking's hut where they found
   ____a. ore.
   ____b. Oliver digging a hole.
   ____c. mining tools hidden in the bushes.
   ____d. a miner hiding behind some bushes.

5. When Elizabeth told her father about her scare with the panther,
   ____a. he told her to stay off the mountain.
   ____b. he decided to leave Templeton.
   ____c. he was eager to get home.
   ____d. he was thankful that Natty had saved her.

6. Squire Doolittle asked the Judge for a court document that would allow him to
   ____a. hunt out of season.
   ____b. make trouble for Natty.
   ____c. search Natty's home.
   ____d. arrest Natty.

7. When the officers arrived at Natty's with a court document that allowed them to search his hut, Natty refused to let them in. Then Natty raised his rifle and took aim at the officers. Next,
   ____a. Billy asked Natty to give himself up.
   ____b. Doolittle and Jotham ran down the mountain.
   ____c. Oliver Edwards went to see the Judge.
   ____d. Natty went to see his lawyer.

8. Judge Temple
   ____a. does not want Natty to go to prison.
   ____b. thinks Natty deserves to go to prison.
   ____c. thinks the laws are too hard on people.
   ____d. thinks Natty should not be held to the law.

9. Another name for this story could be
   ____a. "The Document."
   ____b. "Finding Ore."
   ____c. "The Natives of Templeton."
   ____d. "Natty's Offense."

10. This story is mainly about
   ____a. a poor, helpless, old man who could not be trusted.
   ____b. why Oliver was asked to leave the Temples' home.
   ____c. how changing times and new laws led to Natty's arrest.
   ____d. mining for gold on the Judge's land.

Check your answers with the Key on page 67.

This page may be reproduced for classroom use.

The Arrest

VOCABULARY CHECK

arrest	court	information	officer	person	prison

I. Sentences to Finish
Fill in the blank in each sentence with the correct key word from the box above.

1. Jill went to the library to gather ________________ for her book report.
2. Last night the police came to our door to _______________ my brother.
3. An ____________ of the police department came to our school to teach us about the dangers of using drugs.
4. Jason went to _______________ for stealing a car.
5. Alice went to ______________ to get an order of protection against her husband.
6. Jack is the only _______________ who can get me to laugh when I'm mad!

II. Crossword
Use the words from the box above to fill in the puzzle. Use the meanings below to help you choose the right answer.

Across

1. knowledge or facts
5. a place where justice is served by judge or jury
6. a place where lawbreakers are sent

Down

2. one who holds a public or government office
3. to take into custody
4. a man, woman, or child; a human being

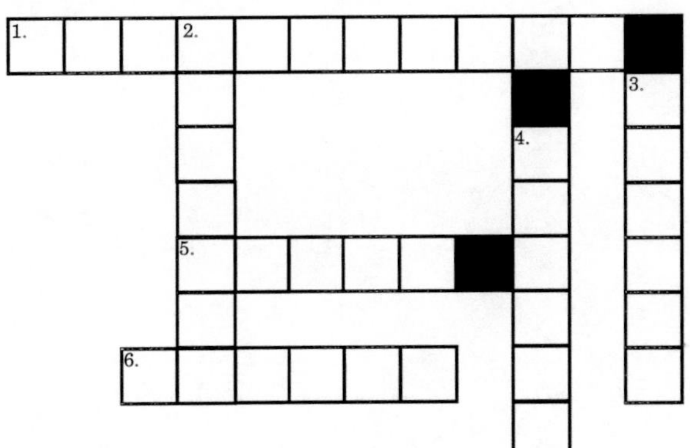

Check your answers with the Key on page 71.

This page may be reproduced for classroom use.

The Trial

PREPARATION

Key Words

comfort	(kum´ fərt)	to ease the grief or sorrow of someone; to cheer *Mary tried to comfort her friend Lisa when Lisa learned she had failed her road test.*
duty	(dü´ tē)	job; work; responsibility *Lee's duty was to raise the flag each morning.*
jail	(jāl)	a place where one is sent for breaking the law *Ronnie was sent to jail for breaking and entering.*
objected	(əb jekt´ əd)	gave reason against something; opposed *Jason objected when his coach took him out of the game.*
perfect	(pėr´ fikt)	without fault; without mistakes *It is impossible to live a perfect life.*
prisoner	(priz´ n ər)	one who is under arrest or held in jail *The prisoner spent three years in jail.*

The Trial

Necessary Words

conscience (kon´ shəns) feelings within you that tell you when you are doing right and warn you of what is wrong

When Linda broke up with Brian, her conscience would not let her keep his ring.

jury (ju̇r´ ē) a group of people chosen to decide a case in a court of law

The jury found the man guilty of stealing a police car.

oxen (ok´ sən) animals used for hard farm work

Mr. Miles bought oxen to help him on the farm.

trial (trī´ əl) a formal examination and deciding of a case in court

The man was on trial for speeding and causing an accident.

People, Places, Things

gunpowder is a powder used in guns to make them fire

the stocks Long ago, people who broke the law were sometimes put in "the stocks" - a heavy wooden frame with holes to put someone's feet through. Sometimes feet and hands were placed in the stocks. The stocks were usually in the center of town where the person could be seen by all the townspeople.

CTR 409-89

The Trial

The prisoner is led into the court.

Preview:
1. Read the name of the story.
2. Look at the picture.
3. Read the sentence under the picture.
4. Read the first six paragraphs of the story.
5. Then answer the following question.

You learned from your preview that Natty was brought into court to

____a. be searched.
____b. answer the charges against him.
____c. see his lawyer.
____d. clear his conscience.

Turn to the Comprehension Check on page 58 for the right answer.

Now read the story.
Read to find out what Natty does after he's put in jail.

The Trial

Judge Temple, Sheriff Jones, some lawyers, and some others met in court. Natty, the prisoner, was brought in by an officer.

Natty had been arrested for pointing a gun at Squire Doolittle and his officers - and for refusing to let the officers search his hut. The hut could never be searched now - Natty had burned it to the ground.

The charges against him were read. Then the Judge said, "Nathaniel Bumppo, what say you to these charges?"

Natty put his head down for a moment. Then he said he was not at fault.

The Judge spoke to Natty's lawyer. "Tell him to answer. Is he *guilty or not guilty?*"

The lawyer talked with Natty. Finally, Natty said, "Guilty, but with a clean conscience."

A trial followed. The jury was seated. Did Squire Doolittle and Kirby have the right to enter Natty's hut to look for the deer? After both sides presented their case, the jury found Natty guilty. The Judge ordered him to be placed in the stocks for one hour. He fined him $100.00, and ordered him to jail for one month. And Natty could not leave jail until the fine was paid.

Natty was angry! He strongly objected. He said he could not pay the fine if he were in jail. And he objected to being locked up for so long. He reminded the Judge that he had just saved his daughter from a hungry panther. But the Judge refused to be moved. And so ended the trial. The prisoner was led to the stocks.

Outside, Natty's feet were placed in the stocks. Ben Pump sat down at the stocks next to Natty. He put his feet in the holes. "If the people want something to see, let them see this - *two* men in the stocks!"

"But I have no order to put *you* in the stocks," said the officer. "Now let me do my duty."

Pump waited for the man to do his duty. Then the officer did as Ben wished. He locked him in the stocks, too.

Elizabeth was very unhappy that Natty was found guilty. She said to her father, "Surely, those laws who would find someone like Leather-stocking guilty are not perfect in themselves."

Her father said that the court had to keep the laws even though they were not perfect.

Elizabeth and Louisa went to the jail to comfort Natty. Outside, they found Edwards with a wagon and oxen. Edwards asked the girls not to tell anyone he was there.

An officer took the girls to see Natty. Elizabeth told Natty that she would give him money to help him build another hut. He told her that it would never be the same. When he heard the oxen outside the jail, he said, "The time has come now."

Elizabeth knew that he was preparing to break out of jail. She asked him not to. She tried to comfort him with her words.

Natty replied, "A month... not a day, not a night, not an hour in jail!"

Elizabeth offered him money to pay his fine, but he refused it. He asked her, instead, to buy some gunpowder for him so he could get some beavers on the mountain.

After the girls left the jail, shouts of *"break-jail," "break-jail!"* were heard in the village.

Edwards had helped Natty break out of jail. Ben went with them. Ben could not leave Natty- his conscience wouldn't let him!

Later that night Elizabeth saw lights on the mountain. The lights were from the men searching for Natty. The search party came back to Templeton empty-handed.

The next morning Elizabeth bought some gunpowder. She went looking for Natty on the mountain. On the way, she met Mohegan. "John, how are you? You have long been away from the village." John talked about his life. John told how white men had made war with their white brothers. They had taken and laid waste the Indian lands. "Daughter," said John, "the Great Spirit made your father with a white skin, and he made my skin with red. But he colored both our hearts with blood."

Elizabeth asked about Mohegan's family. Then she asked, "Who is this Mr. Edwards? Why do you care so much for him, and where does he come from?"

John spread his right arm out with a wave of his hand and said, "As far as your eye can see, it was the land of his. . ."

Just then, smoke rose on the mountain and rolled over their heads.

"What means it, John?" Elizabeth asked, her eyes wide with fear.

A voice called out, "John! Where are you, old Mohegan? The woods are on fire, and you have but a minute to escape!"

It was the voice of Oliver Edwards. He rushed through the dry bushes to their side.

CTR 409-89

The Trial

COMPREHENSION CHECK

Preview Answer:
b. answer the charges against him.

Choose the best answer.

1. Nathaniel Bumppo was being brought up on
____a. one charge.
____b. two charges.
____c. three charges.
____d. four charges.

2. Natty's hut could no longer be searched because
____a. no one was home.
____b. Hiram Doolittle lost the court document that allowed the search.
____c. Billy Kirby had set it on fire.
____d. Natty had burned it to the ground.

3. Natty set fire to his hut
____a. to keep law officers from stepping foot in his home.
____b. to keep warm.
____c. to frighten the villagers.
____d. because he was tired of living there.

4. What did Natty mean when he said he had a clean conscience?
____a. He had just taken a bath.
____b. He felt a need to come clean.
____c. He felt he did not need to present his case.
____d. He felt that he was within his rights to point his rifle at the officers and refuse them entry to his home.

5. When Natty was led to the stocks, who tagged along?
____a. Oliver Edwards
____b. Elizabeth Temple
____c. Ben Pump
____d. Billy Kirby

6. First, Elizabeth and Louisa went to the jail to see Natty. Then, with Oliver's help, Natty broke out of jail. Next,
____a. Natty hid on the mountain.
____b. Elizabeth bought some gunpowder.
____c. the woods were set on fire.
____d. Mohegan and Elizabeth had a long talk.

7. Mohegan told Elizabeth that
____a. he was afraid of the white man.
____b. the white man had laid waste the Indian lands.
____c. red men have great spirits.
____d. they both had the same blood.

8. As Elizabeth talked with Mohegan,
____a. Oliver Edwards listened.
____b. a fire burned in the woods.
____c. a panther circled them.
____d. a great spirit comforted them.

9. Another name for this story could be
____a. "The Perfect Law."
____b. "Beaver Mountain."
____c. "The Search Party."
____d. "Jailbreak."

10. This story is mainly about
____a. Natty's day in court.
____b. why Elizabeth offered to pay for Natty's fine.
____c. how the change in laws caused Natty so much trouble.
____d. why Indians fear the white man.

Check your answers with the Key on page 67.

This page may be reproduced for classroom use.

The Trial

VOCABULARY CHECK

comfort	duty	jail	objected	perfect	prisoner

I. Sentences to Finish
Fill in the blank in each sentence with the correct key word from the box above.

1. When Rick's parents told him to be home by 9:00, he strongly ________________.
2. Fran brought home a great report card. It was almost ________________!
3. The ________________ was caught trying to escape.
4. Sally tried to ________________ the lost child.
5. Doug was sent to ________________ for stealing a car.
6. It is your ________________ to make sure your child goes to school every day.

II. Word Search - All the words from the box above are hidden in the puzzle below. They may be written from left to right, up and down, or on an angle. As you find each word, put a circle around it.

```
O B J A I K C D S
P X D U T Y O U T
R E A S J A M J I
I P R I A L F A A
S O B F I X O I J
O P E F E C R L A
N O B J E C T E D
E C O M F A T D A
R O N D U T E U S
```

Check your answers with the Key on page 71.

This page may be reproduced for classroom use.

Leather-stocking Heads West

PREPARATION

Key Words

death (deth) the end of living
My grandmother's death was very sudden.

lightning (līt´ ning) a flash of light seen in the sky
If you see lightning, try to go indoors.

pioneer (pī´ ə nir´) one who settles in a part of a country, preparing the way for those who come after
Settlers who built homes in the West were pioneers.

shawl (shȯl) a piece of cloth worn on the shoulders or head
Maria's aunt gave her a pretty shawl for her birthday.

thunder (thun´ dər) a loud noise that follows a flash of lightning
The sound of thunder frightens my little sister.

tore (tôr) pulled apart by force
When John climbed the fence, he tore his new pants.

Leather-stocking Heads West

Necessary Words

adopted (ə dopt´ əd) to have taken as one's own
Jason's parents adopted a baby girl.

crackling (krak´ ling) sharp sounds
I heard the dry leaves crackling as Jennifer stepped on them.
I can hear the fire crackling in the fireplace.

graves (grāvz) holes in the ground where the dead are buried
At Christmas, Emily puts flowers on the graves of her mother and grandmother.

pardon (pard´ n) to be set free from punishment
The man became a model prisoner, hoping to receive a pardon.

slick (slik) slippery
The rain and ice made the highway very slick.

People, Places, Things

deerskin a deer's skin, used for clothing

headstone a stone set at the head of a grave

Major Effingham is Oliver's grandfather and the original owner of the lands now held by Judge Temple. After the war, knowing he had lost all his land holdings, he went into the woods, not wanting to face the world as a poor man. Mohegan adopted him and called him "Eagle." Natty and Mohegan had looked out for him all these years. His son, Edward, Judge Temple's good friend, was lost at sea. He left behind a son named Oliver.

Leather-stocking Heads West

Though the flames are circling, Mohegan refuses to leave. He is old and tired, and ready for death.

Preview:
1. Read the name of the story.
2. Look at the picture.
3. Read the sentences under the picture.
4. Read the first five paragraphs of the story.
5. Then answer the following question.

You learned from your preview that Oliver Edwards

____a. will not leave the Indian.
____b. fears for his own life.
____c. fears for Elizabeth's life.
____d. welcomes death.

Turn to the Comprehension Check on page 64 for the right answer.

Now read the story.
Read on to find out who makes it out of the fire.

Leather-stocking Heads West

Edwards rushed up to Mohegan and cried, "It would be sad, indeed, to lose you this way. The flames are circling."

Mohegan, sitting on a log, pointed to Elizabeth. "Save her. Leave John to die." John felt he was too old to move quickly. He would only get in their way. Besides, he was ready for death. In fact, he welcomed it.

Edwards turned and saw Elizabeth. Her face showed great fear. "*Miss Temple!* Is such a death meant for you!"

"No!" cried Elizabeth. "Let us leave here. But, do we leave the Indian?"

"He knows the woods," said Edwards. "He'll find a way out."

Edwards pointed to a rock. "If we reach there before that sheet of fire, we'll be safe."

Heavy smoke was now upon them. Suddenly, there was a crackling noise. "I'm going to die on this mountain," cried Elizabeth.

Edwards led Elizabeth to the rock. Feeling the edges of the rock, Edwards found only slick sides. There was no way to reach the ground below without getting hurt. The rock was too slick.

Edwards ran to get Mohegan's blanket. He tore it into small pieces to make a rope. Next he tore Elizabeth's shawl into strips and added it to the rope. Even with the shawl strips, the rope did not reach the ground.

"It will not do!" cried Elizabeth. "Tell John to move near to us - let us die together."

"I cannot," said Edwards. He thinks his time has come."

"I am going to die," repeated Elizabeth. "If so, it is God's will. But Oliver, you can make it out of here without me. Now, Fly!"

Suddenly they heard a voice. "Girl! Where you be girl?" It was Natty! Natty rushed through the thick smoke to their side. "I've found you," he said to Elizabeth. Wrapping her quickly in his deerskin, he said, "Follow me, and you will escape death!"

"But John! What will become of John?" asked Edwards.

Natty ordered his old friend to leave with them, but he would not. So, Natty threw Mohegan over his shoulder and carried him.

Edwards and Elizabeth followed the old hunter around the crackling fire. Natty knew the woods so well that, even through the thick smoke, he could find his way out.

They came to a safe place near a cave - the cave where Natty had hidden from the law. Natty placed Mohegan against a rock. The Indian began singing. He told Natty good-bye. After a bright flash of lightning and a loud clap of thunder, Mohegan died.

Then heavy rains came and put out the fire. Judge Temple could be heard calling his daughter's name. Richard had sent Billy Kirby and other men from the village to find Leather-stocking.

"Keep off! Keep off, Billy Kirby!" warned Leather-stocking. But the men would not listen.

When the Sheriff and the Judge got to the cave, Richard ordered Natty to turn himself in. But, Natty ran off.

The rain, lightning, and thunder had stopped. The Judge and Richard found Oliver with a white-haired man sitting in a chair by a rock.

"Who is this?" asked the Judge.

"This man," replied Edwards, was the real owner, a pioneer of this land where we now stand."

"Then this," cried the Judge, "is the lost Major Effingham!" He looked at Oliver. "And you. . ."

"He is my grandfather," said Oliver. "Natty has served my grandfather all these years."

"Then you have no Indian blood?" asked the Judge.

"No. Major Effingham was adopted as the son of Mohegan. The Indians gave his adopted son the name of Eagle. They call me 'Young Eagle.'"

Major Effingham, now old and very child-like, was taken back to Templeton. When the old man was put to bed, the Judge asked Edwards to join him in his library. There, the Judge showed Oliver his will. The will explained how he had held onto Major Effingham's land and left a trust to his children and grandchildren.

Oliver and Elizabeth were married a few days before the Major died. Natty turned himself in and went to jail. But shortly after, Natty received a pardon. The pardon made him a free man once again.

One day Oliver and Elizabeth went up the mountain to visit with Natty. They had heard that he was leaving the mountain.

"You've come to see the graves, children, have you?" he asked.

They looked down at the well-kept graves of Mohegan and Major Effingham. Oliver read the headstones out loud. Then he asked Leather-stocking not to go.

"Don't fear for the Leather-stocking," said the old hunter. He waved good-bye and turned to leave.

This was the last time they ever saw him. He went toward the west. He was first in that band of pioneers who would open the way for the march of the nation across America.

Leather-stocking Heads West

COMPREHENSION CHECK

Preview Answer:
c. fears for Elizabeth's life.

Choose the best answer.

1. Mohegan would not leave the woods because
   ____a. he wanted to die with his people.
   ____b. he felt he was too old to outrun the fire.
   ____c. he was a lazy man.
   ____d. he was not alarmed by the fire.

2. First, Edwards led Elizabeth to the rock. Then he made a rope for her to slide down, but it didn't reach the ground. Next,
   ____a. Mohegan died.
   ____b. the rains put out the fire.
   ____c. Natty appeared and led them to safety.
   ____d. the Sheriff sent Billy Kirby to find Natty.

3. Natty
   ____a. would not leave Mohegan behind.
   ____b. gave Mohegan his deerskin to help guard him from the flames.
   ____c. ordered Oliver to lead them out of the woods.
   ____d. carried Elizabeth over his shoulder and led the way out.

4. Natty was able to lead everyone to safety because
   ____a. he knew the woods inside and out.
   ____b. he was a seasoned hunter.
   ____c. he had a map of the mountain.
   ____d. the fire was burning out.

5. Mohegan died
   ____a. at the top of the mountain.
   ____b. in a cave.
   ____c. in Templeton.
   ____d. by the cave where Natty had been hiding from the law.

6. Sheriff Jones ordered Natty to
   ____a. get out of Templeton.
   ____b. keep off the mountain.
   ____c. turn himself in.
   ____d. bury the Indian.

7. All these years, Judge Temple thought Major Effingham
   ____a. had done well for himself.
   ____b. had forgotten his friends and family.
   ____c. had been in jail.
   ____d. had been killed in the war.

8. When the Judge learned that Oliver was the grandson of Major Effingham,
   ____a. he turned over the Major's lands to Oliver.
   ____b. he left Templeton.
   ____c. he pardoned Leather-stocking.
   ____d. he showed Oliver his will and explained everything.

9. Another name for this story could be
   ____a. "Oliver and Elizabeth Get Married."
   ____b. "Natty Leaves the Mountain."
   ____c. "Natty Turns Himself In."
   ____d. "The Last Mohegan."

10. This story is mainly about
   ____a. an old hunter who leaves the place where new laws make it impossible for him to live in the wild.
   ____b. how Natty escaped death.
   ____c. Oliver finding his grandfather.
   ____d. a man called 'Eagle.'

Check your answers with the Key on page 67.

This page may be reproduced for classroom use.

Leather-stocking Heads West

VOCABULARY CHECK

death	lightning	pioneer	shawl	thunder	tore

I. Sentences to Finish

Fill in the blank in each sentence with the correct key word from the box above.

1. My father told me his great-grandfather was a ____________ who helped settle the American West.
2. During the storm, ______________ set fire to a tree in my backyard.
3. When my dog, Rufus, hears the sound of ______________, he hides under the bed.
4. Fran brought a ______________ to the ballgame to keep herself warm.
5. Alex _____________ his shirt when he caught it on a nail.
6. I often wonder if there's life after ________________.

II. Word Use

Put an X next to the best ending for each sentence.

1. A ***shawl***
   ___a. goes well with meatloaf.
   ___b. looks good on you!

2. The sound of ***thunder***
   ___a. often frightens animals.
   ___b. makes me hungry.

3. ***Lightning***
   ___a. can start a fire.
   ___b. is pleasant to listen to.

4. A ***pioneer***
   ___a. is found in the garage.
   ___b. helps to settle a place.

5. Maggie ***tore***
   ___a. her apron.
   ___b. her treasure.

6. ***Death***
   ____a. feels good.
   ____b. brings life to an end.

Check your answers with the Key on page 72.

This page may be reproduced for classroom use.

NOTES

COMPREHENSION CHECK ANSWER KEY

Lessons CTR 409-81 to CTR 409-90

Lesson Number	Question Number										Page Number
	1	2	3	4	5	6	7	8	9	10	
CTR-409-81	c	c	a	d	b	◇ b	d	○ d	△ a	□ c	10
CTR-409-82	c	b	○ b	d	a	○ a	○ d	c	△ b	□ a	16
CTR-409-83	c	d	b	○ a	c	◇ d	a	○ d	△ b	□ c	22
CTR-409-84	○ a	b	○ d	d	c	◇ a	b	b	△ c	□ b	28
CTR-409-85	a	d	◇ b	c	d	○ c	b	d	△ a	□ c	34
CTR-409-86	b	d	d	a	○ a	c	○ b	◇ c	△ c	□ d	40
CTR-409-87	○ a	d	d	c	◇ c	○ b	d	a	△ a	□ b	46
CTR-409-88	b	d	a	c	d	c	◇ b	○ a	△ d	□ c	52
CTR-409-89	b	d	○ a	○ d	c	◇ a	b	b	△ d	□ c	58
CTR-409-90	○ d	◇ c	a	a	d	c	○ d	d	△ b	□ a	64

○ = **Inference (not said straight out, but you know from what is said)**

△ = **Another name for the story**

□ = **Main idea of the story**

◇ = **Sequence (recalling order of events in the story)**

NOTES

VOCABULARY CHECK ANSWER KEY
Lessons CTR 409-81 to CTR 409-83

LESSON NUMBER | **PAGE NUMBER**

81 A COLD WINTER'S NIGHT — 11

I.
1. stocking
2. rifle
3. buck
4. leather
5. settler
6. reins

II.
1. NO
2. YES
3. YES
4. YES
5. NO
6. NO

82 THE HOMECOMING — 17

I.
1. accident
2. servant
3. hut
4. wound
5. area
6. shoulder

II.
1. c
2. e
3. d
4. a
5. b
6. f

83 THE CHURCH SERVICE — 23

I.
1. God
2. friendship
3. mistress
4. future
5. guests
6. pray

II.

<table>
<tr><td></td><td></td><td></td><td></td><td></td><td></td><td>1. G</td><td></td><td></td><td></td></tr>
<tr><td></td><td></td><td></td><td>2. F</td><td>U</td><td>T</td><td>U</td><td>R</td><td>E</td><td></td></tr>
<tr><td></td><td></td><td></td><td>R</td><td></td><td></td><td>E</td><td></td><td></td><td></td></tr>
<tr><td></td><td></td><td></td><td>I</td><td></td><td></td><td>S</td><td></td><td></td><td></td></tr>
<tr><td></td><td></td><td></td><td>E</td><td></td><td></td><td>T</td><td></td><td></td><td></td></tr>
<tr><td></td><td></td><td></td><td>N</td><td></td><td></td><td>S</td><td></td><td></td><td></td></tr>
<tr><td></td><td>3. G</td><td>O</td><td>D</td><td></td><td></td><td></td><td></td><td></td><td></td></tr>
<tr><td></td><td></td><td></td><td>S</td><td></td><td></td><td></td><td></td><td></td><td></td></tr>
<tr><td></td><td></td><td></td><td>H</td><td></td><td></td><td></td><td></td><td></td><td></td></tr>
<tr><td>4. P</td><td></td><td>5. M</td><td>I</td><td>S</td><td>T</td><td>R</td><td>E</td><td>S</td><td>S</td></tr>
<tr><td>R</td><td></td><td></td><td>P</td><td></td><td></td><td></td><td></td><td></td><td></td></tr>
<tr><td>A</td><td></td><td></td><td></td><td></td><td></td><td></td><td></td><td></td><td></td></tr>
<tr><td>Y</td><td></td><td></td><td></td><td></td><td></td><td></td><td></td><td></td><td></td></tr>
</table>

VOCABULARY CHECK ANSWER KEY
CTR 409-84 to CTR 409-86

LESSON NUMBER		PAGE NUMBER
84	THE BOLD DRAGOON BAR-ROOM	29

I.

1. action
2. turkey
3. settle
4. sheriff
5. purpose
6. peace

II.

T	P	E	A	L	A	C	T	S
U	P	A	C	T	I	O	N	H
R	E	U	S	E	T	T	L	E
K	A	I	R	F	F	P	L	R
A	C	T	T	P	F	U	E	I
L	E	P	U	R	O	R	C	F
T	U	R	K	E	Y	S	P	F
P	S	H	E	R	F	F	E	P

85 THE JUDGE'S ASSISTANT 35

I.

1. claim
2. sugar
3. spent
4. reminded
5. suggested
6. skill

86 SPRING IN THE VILLAGE 41

I.

1. rough
2. spear
3. pigeons
4. accept
5. pride
6. agreed

II.

1. YES
2. NO
3. YES
4. NO
5. YES
6. NO

VOCABULARY CHECK ANSWER KEY
Lessons CTR 409-87 to CTR 409-89

LESSON NUMBER | **PAGE NUMBER**

87 BREAKING THE LAW **47**

I.
1. sight
2. greeted
3. protection
4. August
5. January
6. leaped

II.
1. f
2. c
3. d
4. e
5. a
6. b

88 THE ARREST **53**

I.
1. information
2. arrest
3. officer
4. prison
5. court
6. person

II.

1. I	N	F	2. O	R	M	A	T	I	O	N	■
			F						■		3. A
			F						4. P		R
			I						E		R
			5. C	O	U	R	T	■	R		E
			E						S		S
		6. P	R	I	S	O	N		O		T
									N		

89 THE TRIAL **59**

I.
1. objected
2. perfect
3. prisoner
4. comfort
5. jail
6. duty

II.

O	B	J	A	I	K	C	D	S
P	X	D	U	T	Y	O	U	T
R	E	A	S	J	A	M	J	I
I	P	R	I	A	L	F	A	A
S	O	B	F	I	X	O	I	J
O	P	E	F	E	C	R	L	A
N	O	B	J	E	C	T	E	D
E	C	O	M	F	A	T	D	A
R	O	N	D	U	T	E	U	S

VOCABULARY CHECK ANSWER KEY
Lesson CTR 409-90

LESSON NUMBER		PAGE NUMBER
90	**LEATHER-STOCKING HEADS WEST**	**65**

I.	1. pioneer	***II.***	1. b
	2. lightning		2. a
	3. thunder		3. a
	4. shawl		4. b
	5. tore		5. a
	6. death		6. b